Library and Archives Canada Cataloguing in Publication

Title: Nonna & the girls next door / Gianna Patriarca and Ellie Arscott.
Other titles: Nonna and the girls next door
Names: Patriarca, Gianna, author. | Arscott, Ellie, 1974- illustrator.
Description: Illustrated by Ellie Arscott.
Identifiers: Canadiana (print) 2022019288X | Canadiana (ebook) 20220192898 |
    ISBN 9781772602494 (hardcover) | ISBN 9781772602500 (EPUB)
Classification: LCC PS8581.A6665 N66 2022 | DDC jC813/.54—dc23

Printed and bound in Canada

Second Story Press gratefully acknowledges the support of the Ontario Arts Council and the Canada Council for the Arts for our publishing program. We acknowledge the financial support of the Government of Canada through the Canada Book Fund.

Published by
Second Story Press
20 Maud Street, Suite 401
Toronto, Ontario, Canada
M5V 2M5
www.secondstorypress.ca

Nonna and The Girls Next Door

Gianna Patriarca and
Ellie Arscott

Second Story Press

The girls next door
have everything.

They have a cat named Paws and a dog named Jake. They have a turtle who lives in an old plastic swimming pool under the big maple tree.

The girls next door have pink and purple bikes
and shiny new scooters they ride in the schoolyard
behind our house.

The girls next door have a tree house with a real wooden ladder and a tiny window with a striped red and yellow curtain. When the wind blows the leaves dance all around the tree house.

They climb up and have tea parties with their dolls and their stuffed toys. They drink pretend tea from little ceramic cups. The wind sneaks in under the red and yellow curtain to keep them cool.

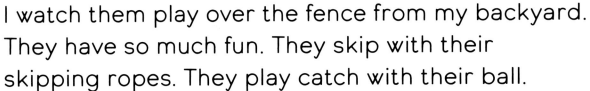

I watch them play over the fence from my backyard. They have so much fun. They skip with their skipping ropes. They play catch with their ball.

Sometimes they hold hands and swing in fast circles,

round and round and round

until they fall down on the grass laughing.

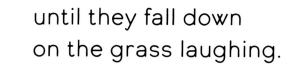

The girls next door have everything.
Most of all, the girls next door have each other.

Sometimes I wish I was one of the girls next door.

I live on Grace Street with my mommy, my daddy, and my nonna. My nonna takes care of me when Mommy and Daddy go to work and when I come home from school.

The girls next door go to daycare after school and in the summer they go to day camp. I want to go to daycare too where there are lots and lots of children to play with, but then my nonna would be very lonely.

My nonna says she will play with me. But my nonna is old and she can't swing round and round in fast circles. Her knees hurt and she can't skip with a rope, or ride a bicycle, or climb a wooden ladder.

Nonna says she isn't too old to tell me stories and to bake my favorite biscotti.

I help her mix the dough with butter and sugar and eggs. We make animal biscotti. They are my favorite.

I make a cat that looks
like Paws and a dog
that looks like Jake.

Nonna likes to make stars and moons and angels.

While we make the biscotti,
Nonna tells me stories of
when she was a little girl.
Some of the stories are funny.
We laugh together a lot.

When she was little, she lived on a farm in another country far away.

She learned how to milk a cow and feed rabbits and chickens.

I feed the birds that come into our garden in the summertime.

Nonna asks if I would like to make some biscotti for the girls next door. We make some that look like the turtle.

The girls next door love my nonna's biscotti and say, "Thank you. You are so lucky to have a nonna, especially one who can bake biscotti."

Nonna looks from our kitchen window. She has a big smile on her face.

I like the girls next door.
The girls next door have everything.

But they don't
have my nonna.